THE DEVIL'S MEMOIR

SEX, SMOKE, AND SCRIPTURE

BY

SEAN PATRICK PAGE

Table of Contents

Introduction 1

12-24-2024 4

The year of the Lord 4

   Enjoy life today Yesterday Is gone & TOMORROW May never
come 4

4-19-1981 8

The year of the Lord 8

9-11-2001 11

The year of the Lord 11

5-25-1979 14

The year of the Lord 14

11-23-1944 17

The year of the Lord 17

   A Miracle in the Ashes 18

TODAY 19

The year of the Lord 19

   The Preparation of the ARMY OF DARKNESS 19

7-7-1976 22

The year of the Lord 22

2500 BC 25

The year of the Lord 25

1-5-2025 28

The year of the Lord 28

1-21-1919 34

The year of the Lord 34

5-23-1618 to 10-24-1648 36

The year of the Lord 36

September 8--11, 9 AD 43

The year of the Lord 43

1-30-1945 47

The year of the Lord 47

12-7-1941 53

The year of the Lord 53

1-28-1986 58

The year of the Lord 58

    The Holy Ghost: Igor Petrov, King of Standing Still 59

    The "Holy Trinity" of Soviet Catastrophes 60

4-26-1986 61

The year of the Lord 61

4-1-1993 to 10-10-1993 67

The year of the Lord 67

Today 69

The year of the Lord 69

    How It Played Out 75

    The Legend Behind the Name 78

9-28-1982 81

The year of the Lord 81

1029–1291 86

The Year of the Lord 86

    Meet Me at The Diner 86

5-6-1937 89

The year of the Lord 89

    The Night We Were Destroyed by Led Zeppelin 89

    Final Thoughts 90

    Meet the Trifecta 90

1-21-2025 93

The Year of The Lord 93

    The Wonderful Los Angeles 2025 Fires 93

Wherever You Are At 95

The Year of the Lord 95

About the Author 99

Dedication

1

Dedicated to wife and kids

Disclaimer:

Within these pages, you'll find a sprinkle of irreverence, a dash of profanity, and more than a few moments that might make your grandmother clutch her pearls. If you proceed, it's on you, we did our part.

Introduction

What if the world as you know it is teetering on the edge of an unseen battle? What if the forces that shape our fate—both divine and malevolent—are closer than we dare to acknowledge?

The Devil's Memoir is not just a novel; it's a revelation. Drawing from theology, history, and the chilling realities of our modern world, Dr. Sean Patrick Page crafts a gripping supernatural thriller that challenges the very fabric of faith, morality, and perception. At its core, this book forces us to confront an unsettling truth: if we instinctively thank God when tragedy is averted, why do we so often overlook the existence of evil?

Through the story of Mary MacNamara—a woman entangled in a reality where nothing is as it seems—*The Devil's Memoir* explores the eerie crossroads of science and faith, fate and free will, angels and demons. With a narrative steeped in meticulous research and firsthand experience, Patrick Page masterfully blurs the lines between the tangible and the supernatural, urging readers to question not only the world around them but also the unseen battles waged in the shadows.

This is more than a story—it's a call to awareness. A chilling reminder that the devil is closer than we think.

12-24-2024

The year of the Lord

Enjoy life today Yesterday Is gone & TOMORROW May never come

Mary MacNamara noticed the plaque on the back of the bathroom door while providing a urine specimen for the nurse—required at every damn visit. Fertility clinics were a godsend, yet they had their protocols. A necessary evil. But still, a pain in the ass.

That's so, so, so beautiful, she thought, her breath catching. Mom had the exact same plaque in their kitchen, right above the range. It had always been there—watching over every meal, every conversation, every steaming cup of her mother's rich, dark coffee. So much coffee. Small meals, big meals, shared with family, friends, and the occasional unexpected guest.

TOMORROW MAY NEVER COME.
A lump formed in her throat. Maybe she would like this clinic. It felt... familiar.

She was scheduled for a brief consultation with Nurse Elizabeth.

More inconsistencies.

The wall art in the hallway—intended to be inspirational— showed a stylized crucifixion scene. But the symbolism was... odd. The inscription—INRI—was missing. No crown of thorns. And the lighting in the piece seemed reversed. Christ faced east, the crowd west, the whole thing subtly off-kilter.

At first glance, reverent. But something didn't sit right. As though someone had tried too hard and landed just shy of sincere.

A strange chill ran through Mary.

The air thickened—still, heavy. Something about the moment felt electric, like a thunderstorm waiting to break.

Then the door opened.

Dr. Nicholas entered, coffee in hand. His presence was commanding, yet disturbingly effortless. The staff jokingly called him **Old Nick**—a nickname that always seemed to carry more than a trace of mystery.

He was dressed casually, at ease. His smile—was it a smile? A grin? A smirk? Whatever it was, it walked a fine line between charm and danger.

Mary's breath caught.

For the first time in her life, she *felt* it—truly *felt* it. That primal, electric awareness of being a woman. A kind of raw, visceral power. Sensual. Intoxicating. And the way he looked at her... as if she were already his.

If he wanted her, she'd let him.

Any way he wanted.

"So," he said, flipping open her file, "ready to take over the world? Or at least, Chicago?"

Sixteen months later. After multiple IVF cycles.

Success.

Mary gave birth to a beautiful baby girl—eight pounds, six ounces. Jenny.

She had no idea.

No idea that Jenny's biological father was the doctor himself.

Nor that she had over 1,700 half-siblings, scattered across the city. All conceived at this very clinic. Over the past decade.

It wasn't an error. Not a mix-up.

It had been intentional. Planned. Every step.

Dr. Nicholas had ensured it—with precision. Each time, with quiet confidence. A man with his own definition of legacy. His version of immortality.

But Mary got what she wanted. A child born of longing. Of hope.

Didn't she?

The war raged on, and strength left the bodies of the fallen. The dead remained where they had fallen, left to be reclaimed by the earth.

In a dimly lit tent reserved for officers of rank, Publius lay at the threshold of two worlds. Pain rippled through him in waves, searing and unrelenting—until, suddenly, it wasn't.

A figure emerged from the shadows—calm, composed, unbothered by the stench of blood and iron that clung to the air. He said nothing. Simply approached, placing his hand over Publius's open wound.

And just like that, the pain was gone.

Then, the man leaned forward, pressing a kiss to his forehead. When he finally spoke, his voice was both commanding and quiet, almost reverent:

"You've been given a second chance. Use it wisely."

And then—he vanished.

When the battlefield was finally cleared, the dead were buried or left to the earth. Yet Publius survived. Against all odds.

He became a decorated hero, though always surrounded by whispers. A man who had suffered mortal wounds—yet walked, spoke, and lived as if untouched.

He never stopped looking for the stranger who saved him. Wanting to thank him. To understand.

But according to every surviving officer, every field medic, and every nurse...

There had been no doctors on that side of the line.

4-19-1981

The year of the Lord

"Ya mon! Want a Red Stripe? Special deal just for you! Or maybe something else, monnnnn! Appleton Rum, perhaps?"

It was Easter Sunday in Ocho Rios, Jamaica. A sweltering 102 degrees. The Silver Seas Hotel—a hidden gem—offered a quiet refuge far from the frenzy of all-inclusive resorts where tourists were squeezed for every last nickel. Its private beach could only be reached by descending a narrow staircase carved into the cliffside. Another led directly into the Caribbean.

Here, in the solace of the sea breeze, a local man sat grinning ear to ear, his warm eyes twinkling with history and humor.

"Ya mon, take a seat and hear me out," he said, with a chuckle in his voice. "My people have been through a lot. First the Spanish, then the British came in 1655 during the Anglo-Spanish War. We endured. And we still here, strong as ever. So if you're enjoying the view, maybe leave a little tip, yeah?"

John Matthew McConnack laughed, genuinely charmed. A young man from Confluence, Pennsylvania—a small rural town near the Maryland and West Virginia border—he was a long way from home. Life in Confluence was a world apart from this tropical paradise. The Southwest Pennsylvania Railroad—one of the busiest freight lines in the continental U.S.—cut right through his backyard.

It was that sudden awareness—the kind that makes your neck hair stand on end—that hit him.

Something felt... off. Terribly off.

There was a presence nearby. Deliberate. Predatory.

Then—it happened.

As the saying goes, your life flashes before your eyes.

The sand shark struck with a jolt, brushing against him like a freight train underwater. The force tore through his wetsuit, shredding flesh. Blood clouded the sea around him, carried by the current, a silent signal that rippled outward.

The shark circled back, tasting the disturbance.

Was it just a test bite?

Or was this the beginning of something worse?

A kill.

John's survival instincts kicked in. He grabbed his dive knife, ready to aim for the shark's eyes. With his other hand, he purged his regulator—releasing a blast of bubbles to confuse and distract the hunter in the deep.

Above the surface, a nearby fishing boat had been watching. The violent churn of bubbles told them everything they needed to know.

Trouble.

He wasn't just a patient. He was a miracle.

The nurses whispered about him—equal parts awe and curiosity.

The South African surgeon from Doctors Without Borders had become a legend of sorts. Tall, striking, with Dutch and French roots, his presence was magnetic—equal parts mystery and mastery.

When he finally arrived, his expression was unreadable. He shook John's hand firmly.

"Ya mon. We almost lost you."

His tone was smooth, calm—like he was chatting about a missed flight, not a near-death shark attack.

"I had plans to watch the match and enjoy a cold one," the doctor added with a smirk. "Didn't happen. So, now you owe me."

John managed a weak laugh. "How can I ever pay you back?"

The doctor paused, thoughtful. Then, with a knowing smile, replied:

"Just get well. Marry that sweetheart we all met. Start a good life."

9-11-2001

The year of the Lord

Elizabeth had been in labor for twelve hours. It was her first—a baby girl, to be named Lucy. Or, as she and her husband had promised in prayer, Lucky—because she had been told she'd never conceive, let alone carry a child to term. And yet, here they were.

Family members crowded the room, their excitement electric. Balloons bobbed near the ceiling, gift baskets had arrived early, and well-wishers drifted in and out, their joy impossible to contain. The anesthesiologist had performed what Elizabeth now considered a divine act—an epidural, sending waves of blessed relief through her body. *Magic,* she thought. *Pure magic.*

Then, as if time itself had halted, the entire maternity unit fell silent.

Muffled gasps echoed in the hallway.
"Oh my God..."

A deep, eerie stillness blanketed the room.

All eyes turned to the television mounted in the corner. The first images of what would become one of the darkest days in American history—September 11th—flickered across the screen. That bright, clear morning, which had begun like any other—with people grabbing coffee, heading to work, kissing loved ones goodbye—had turned into a living nightmare.

Suddenly, Elizabeth cried out.

Blood pooled beneath her—a clear sign of an acute placental abruption. Then came the sharp, unrelenting tone of the fetal monitor.

Flatline.
No heartbeat.

The attending physician called for an emergency cesarean, but all anesthesiologists were in the operating rooms, assisting with critical cases related to the national emergency. A surgical delivery wasn't an option.

Then the traveling OB stepped in.

He was an older doctor from Germany, visiting on a short-term rotation. Unlike many of his younger colleagues, he had long ago mastered the art of forceps delivery—training in remote villages where operating rooms weren't always an option, and emergencies like this one were all too common.

With a calm forged by decades of experience, he worked with precision and speed. The room held its breath.

And then—

A single, sharp cry.

The newborn inhaled again. And again.

Then came the screaming. Loud, relentless, and glorious.

Elizabeth burst into tears. Around her, the room—still haunted by the morning's tragedy—breathed out in collective relief.

The doctor, composed amid the emotional storm, gave a small nod and turned to leave.

But before he could walk out the door, Elizabeth reached for him.

5-25-1979

The year of the Lord

It was Elk Grove Village, a Chicago suburb nestled along the edge of O'Hare International Airport—one of the busiest in the world. The day was picture-perfect: clear skies, warm but not stifling, and a Friday that felt full of possibility.

Chris G. was hell-bent on striking out Jimmy C. Their childhood rivalry ran deep—twisted in years of being next-door neighbors, navigating the awkward aftermath of their parents' divorces, and, to their horror, watching those same parents briefly date each other. Maybe even *before* the divorces. To top it off, they had to tolerate each other every single day in gym class at Clearmont Grade School.

The usual gang was there: Sean, Cleary, Jamie, Tim, Dave, Mike, and a few stragglers who always showed up once the game got rolling. And then there was Todd—solid guy. His mom was a banker up the street, his dad ran the local park district, and his sisters—the older one and the younger—were the kind who wore tube tops and short shorts, casually driving the neighborhood boys to distraction.

Todd, for his part, smoked a lot of weed, and his house was a constant soundtrack of Zeppelin, Hendrix, and Emerson, Lake & Palmer, blasted at full volume until the cops inevitably showed up.

You got used to the noise. The constant roar of planes overhead shaking the walls was just background music in Elk Grove. Like a barking dog, a squeaky door, or a crying baby. The

Dairy Queen never changed—only the faces behind the counter did.

Then came the day everything stopped.

It was a crash—an engine failure, they later said. Just off the edge of the airport. Two hundred seventy-three lives lost in an instant. Two hundred seventy-one on board. Two in their homes, caught in the fire—most likely asleep.

We were kids. Morbidly curious. So we went.

Todd grabbed his keys. We piled into his car and headed toward the smoke. We parked where we could and ran the rest of the way on foot. From across the street, we saw the wreckage: the torn fuselage, black smoke, crushed trailers. First responders everywhere. And then—we saw them.

The bodies.

It was real. Staggering. Quiet chaos in motion.

They kept coming. And then we saw something we couldn't explain.

A group of responders carried what looked like a lifeless man, dropping him gently onto a tarp alongside others. Just minutes ago, these people had been alive—mothers, fathers, children, neighbors. Now, they were names that would fill the headlines the next day.

Then a firefighter stepped forward. He was tall, broad-shouldered, calm amid the madness. He knelt beside the man, placed a single hand on his chest...

And the man sat up.

We watched, frozen. They exchanged words—muffled by sirens and the rising murmur of emergency crews.

Then, just as silently as he came, the firefighter stood, turned, and walked back into the wreckage. Into the smoke.

We never learned his name.

11-23-1944

The year of the Lord

The Cathedral and the Miracle

The Cathedral of Our Lady of Strasbourg, a masterpiece of Rayonnant Gothic architecture with subtle Romanesque undertones, stood faintly illuminated by the flickering glow of candlelight. Its stained-glass windows—an intricate mosaic of radiant hues forged from elemental oxides—seemed to weep quietly, as if aware that peace was finally on the horizon.

Crafted by generations of devoted artisans in the 13th and 14th centuries, these windows had borne witness to both triumph and tragedy. Miraculously, they had endured.

The cathedral had withstood the advance of Hitler's armies, escaping full-scale destruction. And though Allied bombings swept across Europe in waves, seeking to dismantle the Nazi war machine, the church stood firm—a quiet testament to human resilience in a time of unimaginable loss.

On November 22, 1944, General Philippe Leclerc de Hautecloque and the French First Army received their orders. The following day, they entered Strasbourg and raised the Free French tricolor above the beloved cathedral. Though German forces attempted desperate counterattacks, the tide had turned. The regime was unraveling.

Europe would begin the long road to healing—physically, economically, and spiritually.

He briefed Philippe on Peter's condition—the burns, the amputation, the challenges ahead. Peter simply grinned.

"I'll get through it," he said matter-of-factly. "I'm named after a saint, after all."

A Miracle in the Ashes

Later, as they sat with lukewarm hospital coffee, the doctor leaned in close, his tone hushed and deliberate.

"There's something you should know," he said. "Peter was brought in... gone."

Philippe went still.

"Massive blood loss," the doctor continued. "We applied a tourniquet, gave multiple transfusions—but there was nothing. No pulse. No breath. Then..." He paused. "I touched his forehead. A few times. And suddenly—his eyes fluttered open. Just like that."

The general stared, silently asking the question that had no answer.

"When he stabilized, I told him he had a long life ahead. That he'd see children, grandchildren... and that he'd better behave, heal fast, and make it count."

Peter, ever himself—even in pain—had smirked.

"Doctor's orders?" he asked.

TODAY

The year of the Lord

The Preparation of the ARMY OF DARKNESS

How are you doing? Call me Bob, or Steve—heck, even Lucy. That one's short for Lucifer. Has a certain flair, doesn't it? Rolls off the tongue like silk. And yes, I have a few other aliases: The Adversary, The Prince of Darkness, Abaddon, and, of course, Satan. Pick your poison.

The last one—Prince of Darkness? The ladies seem to love that one. Something about it makes them melt—less talkative, more attentive. Sometimes, a little too attentive.

Here's what always tickles me: the idea that you humans were made in "His" image. Hilarious. And yet that's all you got—an image. Let's talk about the things that didn't quite stick: clarity, discipline, grace. Let's just say it's a mixed bag.

I mean, seriously. Look around. Incest, corruption, child neglect, infidelity, abuse, wars... You're an absolute disaster, a glorious mess of contradictions. But adorable, in a chaotic kind of way.

So why this little chat before the journey begins? Simple: I'll be your guide.

I should probably apologize in advance if this leaves you questioning everything you thought you knew about that higher power you call Father. But hey—no rush. I'll go slow. I know your minds can only handle so much.

And if by the end of this, you're not upset, not just a little furious about the cards you've been dealt—well, stay on the path He paved for you. That whole "free will" thing? Sure. Let's go with that.

But we both know how this ends.

I will win. I will control. I will turn your fractured little world into something far more interesting.

And when it's over, when the dust clears, I'll be waiting.

People living among livestock, nestled beside someone they believed to be the world's savior—what a parallel to the human condition. Wretched, beautiful, complicated.

History kept repeating: Reformation, Holy Wars, empires rising and falling. All in the name of righteousness. All accompanied by suffering.

Let's talk about Gustavus Adolphus, King of Sweden. A brilliant commander, remembered as Adolphus the Great. He changed the face of war with tactics still studied today. But in the end? Like so many, war swallowed him whole.

The Battle of Lützen. Trying to rally his troops, he rode straight into the Imperial cavalry. Three bullets. Off his horse. Gone. His body wasn't recovered until the battlefield quieted, 16 hours later.

They said he knew when that first bullet struck. Then the second. Then the third. And yet—he kept going. Some warriors are like that.

It wasn't love. Not even intimacy.

It was something raw, transactional. Survival. Food, shelter, protection.

But the moment stayed with her. Not the act. Not the strength. Not the heat of his breath. It was what he said after:

"You're mine. Forever. And so is my child."

The words branded her soul. Not out of fear. But because she knew, in that instant, that it was true.

Then came the shots. Two of them. Sharp. Loud.

It was two young rebels from the IRA. They gunned down two Royal Irish Constabulary officers, and history took a new path.

As it often does, the real trigger was unresolved pain. Generational injustice. Quiet resentment. Unseen scars.

Then came the spark.

Ironically, for all the rage behind it, this war didn't drag on forever. Two years, five months, two weeks, and six days.

The Government of Ireland Act passed. A truce signed.

And what came of it?

Well—that depends on who you ask.

7-7-1976

The year of the Lord

It had been one hell of a week—an even crazier weekend.

The American Bicentennial.

Two hundred years of stars, stripes, and spectacle. Victorious in two world wars. Bloodied in Korea and Vietnam. Six landings on the moon—twelve men leaving their boots on that cold, orbiting rock. We planted six American flags where no one had gone before—bold, proud, defiant.

And through it all, Don McLean's *American Pie* hummed from AM 890 radio—WLS Chicago.

There were burgers, fries, and beer at Cedar Lake. Sunburned shoulders. Bonfires lining the shoreline. The scent of something sweet and smoky curling through the air. And all those boys—each one just a little too perfect, a little too far out of reach.

Or so she thought.

But then came another beer. The sunset. That mix of music, sweat, and summer haze. And suddenly, she found herself leaning into the very moment her mom had warned her about since middle school.

It was okay. He was kind of an ass. She didn't finish. But hey—it was the goddamn '70s.

"Careful trimming your bikini line," he said casually, eyes locked on hers as he adjusted his gloves. "Ingrown hairs are a pain."

A pause. A smirk.

"Wouldn't want to ruin that Mona Lisa smile." His tone was warm, oddly soothing. Too smooth.

"Use a mirror. Take your time. Avoid any nicks near sensitive skin."

Another beat.

"But really—looks good. Very... neat."

Her breath caught, but she wasn't sure why.

Then came the speculum. He warmed it in his hands— something she only realized later.

He explained what he was doing, carefully, clinically. And yet… something didn't feel right.

There was an awareness—a heightened, strange response from her body she couldn't quite explain. And when the exam was done, he lingered just a moment too long. Adjusting. Straightening.

Neatening.

Her body reacted against her will—tightened abdomen, flushed skin, the kind of physiological response that left her deeply unsettled.

She didn't go back to the beach. But she did return to Student Health.

Once. Twice. Again.

Each time, framed as "treatment." Each time, she left confused, dazed, and conflicted.

But the real alarm came after. The next day, her body changed. A strange kind of discharge. Too much. Too persistent.

She brushed it off.

Then—two weeks later.

A positive pregnancy test.

It had to be the guy at the lake, right?

Had to be.

Because a doctor? A medical professional?

No. No way. That couldn't happen.

...Could it?

2500 BC

The year of the Lord

Yeah, a little curveball. Scratching your head? Well, technically, the calendar starts at Year Zero. LOL. Or wait— now it's 4 to 6 BC? Make it make sense. And which genius among humanity decided *they* get to define facts and rearrange the cosmic clock?

Let's rewind for a sec. The Big Bang? That was 13.7 billion years ago. Your cozy little blue dot—third rock from the Sun— showed up about 3.5 billion years in. Give or take. But sure, let's keep arguing over dates while the universe laughs.

So, who's really in charge here? That ever-elusive creator figure you've been praying to for centuries? The one who, depending on which version you read, has been making up rules as He goes?

"Made in His image"? Yeah... let's just say, that sounds more like creative branding than fact.

And the messenger? The chosen one who keeps showing up in different stories across different eras? Always with the same job: help humans stop screwing up. On someone else's orders, of course.

Anyway, let's not get ahead of ourselves. We'll get to Egypt. And no, I'm not just talking pyramids and sand. I'm talking real history. Who built them, why they were built, how old they really are—and who that stunningly well-preserved mummy actually was.

But that's for later. Right now? I need a drink. Maybe two. Because I can already see the "what-the-hell-is-he-saying" look forming on your face. Let's take it slow.

She lost her scalp. Her arm. And along with them, her identity—her confidence, her dreams, her place in society. In one brutal moment, she became invisible. Unmentionable.

And that's where I came in. You're not-so-average rescuer.

Or let's say—pharaoh with a flair for timing.

I brought her in. Gave her food, safety, a place. Look, I even cleaned. Hunted. Did the whole support system thing.

And in return? She became mine.

To be fair, she was amazing. Grateful, even—just to be wanted again. The trick? Positioning. Keep her facing forward, angled just right. Out of sight, out of mind. The reminders of the trauma didn't exactly set the mood.

Sorry. Honesty's kind of my thing.

Five years. Three kids. Then—my cue to exit. That's just how I move.

Spare me the moral outrage.

She got what she needed—respect, a family, a fresh start.

And me?

Well, I never leave empty-handed.

1-5-2025

The year of the Lord

Quick side note.

These are just glimpses of the chaos I've set in motion. Mere fragments of a grand, beautifully twisted design.

You see, my infernal army—the one destined to bring about the final reckoning, the ultimate clash that resets the scales—is built on a single, unstoppable truth:

Every one of my descendants is born with dual blood.

Half of their essence carries the powerful trace of my darker nature—tainted, sharp, unrelenting. The other half? Unfortunately, human. Fragile, imperfect, and molded in that all-too-familiar form. A design flaw, really. But that's where the genius lies.

Because these children—every single one of them—are drawn to each other. Pulled by something deeper than instinct. Fated to find one another. To come together not in love, but in power. And when they unite, they birth something entirely new.

Something unfiltered. Uncompromising.

A being of pure darkness.

No dilution. No weakness.

The true architects of the world I intend to build.

Hell on Earth? Yeah. That's just the beginning.

Oh no, I play a much bigger game.

It's not just the ones born of my seed. No. It's also the ones I've *saved*. The ones I've *resurrected*. The ones who had already breathed their last breath—until *I* gave it back to them.

When I bring them back, when I reanimate their pitiful corpses, I don't just return their lives—I *infect* them. Every cell in their bodies. Their flesh, their blood, their bones. Their cursed fate.

Which means every child they bring into this world carries my darkness.

Half-demon. Half me.

And just like the rest, they'll seek each other out. They'll find each other. And when they do? When they *merge*?

The cycle is complete.

The bastards become pure evil.

Game on.

And F.P.

That's fair play.

Trust me—it's one hell of a party.

LMF'AO.

You know what? Don't judge. I'm the f***ing Devil.

Ancient Egypt. Pyramids. That's where we'll start.

You mortals love to think you're the wisest beings on the planet. If that were true, explain the self-inflicted mayhem you keep diving headfirst into. Seriously, do you really believe they cut, quarried, transported, and stacked 2.5 million blocks—each weighing 2.5 tons—in just 20 years?

OMG. LMAO. No, wait—LMFAO.

And sure, the Sphinx is the same age as the pyramids. And Egypt was always a desert. And the Nile was the only waterway. And everything looked exactly the same then as it does today. Right.

But hey, you're the *children of progress*, right? So obviously, you're all-knowing, flawless, and just dripping with insight and compassion.

Sorry, can't help the sarcasm. Some things just *need* to be said.

Back to the girl. Her Egyptian name was Noor—meaning light.
Ironic, huh?

See, when you're building a monstrosity for a guy you've never seen—who never speaks to anyone, demands constant praise, and has sixteen wives—you're not exactly motivated to give a sh*t. Add to that 112-degree heat, barely any food or water, and sleeping in a cramped space with half the planet—who smell, steal your bread, and sleep-talk about the one that got away—and mistakes are bound to happen.

That's exactly what happened to Noor.

The ropes weren't inspected. One snapped. A pillar came crashing down.

Well.

There was always DNA.

And soon, she'd know.

Questions she hadn't asked. Questions she wasn't even sure she wanted the answers to.

He excused himself, then returned—with good news and bad.

"I think I know what's going on," he said. "It's Trich. Easily treated. We'll still run the rest of the panel to be sure, but there's a newer treatment we can try today. Just a few seconds, and you should start feeling better by tomorrow."

She nodded.

"It's a topical antibiotic with a pH stabilizer," he explained, pulling on gloves. "I'll apply it directly, and we'll get you on your way."

She should've felt embarrassed. Nervous, even. But instead, she felt… anticipation. This time, she was ready. This time, she leaned in.

She made small talk—not to distract, but to extend the moment. To hold onto it just a little longer.

And when it happened?

Oh, did it happen.

Hard. Deep. Again. And again.

He had to know. He *had* to.

What came next? That was the price you paid. A big, fat, itchy, painful price.

Discharge. Odor. The relentless, infuriating itch.

Yep. Mom had warned her.

So off to Student Affairs she went—the free clinic, her last resort.

Looking back, what happened there *should* have felt clinical, transactional. But in that moment? It was something else. Seductive. Erotic. Intense in ways she hadn't expected. Maybe even more than that reckless beach encounter that led to this whole mess.

The nurse did her thing—slow intake, awkward questions. Then the doctor walked in. Calm. Tired, but collected. The kind of presence that settled the room without a word.

He explained everything clearly. What it could be. What tests they'd run. The empirical treatment in the meantime. His voice was steady. Grounding.

And then came the exam.

His first comment caught her off guard. It was subtle. Uninvited. But strangely... charged.

Meanwhile... somewhere far away:

It butchered the land.

That breathtaking countryside—its rolling green hills, rocky cliffs, and mist-covered coastal towns—was ripped apart. Torn into two hostile regions, both claiming the same roots.

Up north? A self-governing, crown-loyal state. Down south? The so-called Free State.

But "free" was a stretch. Because buried in the fine print of that drunkenly signed agreement, six counties remained tethered to their former rulers.

LMFAO.

And you wonder why every Irish pub still houses at least one bitter, ranting drunk.

Oh, and the cost? A casual 2,500 soldiers. A thousand civilians. Give or take.

God's children, of course.

But hey—for a brief flicker in time—they had their little slice of paradise.

A place called Ireland. Tease, tease, tease.

1-21-1919

The year of the Lord

The Anglo-Irish War—or as many a drunken Irishman would call it, the Irish War of Independence—began as most days did on the Emerald Isle: gray, wet, damp, and overcast, with that relentless, biting breeze. People lit cigarettes, shielding them from the misty air as best they could.

And then there was Mary McPherson—slightly overweight, but still sexy in that natural, windswept Irish way—pushing a stroller with one child inside and two more clinging to her hands. The usual routine: banker, butcher, bakery. Thick, calorie-laden Irish bread was on the list. Mary loved her children, no conditions, no exceptions. She fed them, clothed them, raised them—alone.

Why? Because he never had time.

He never set anything aside—not money, not space, not even plans. Still latched onto his mother's apron strings at 24. Never once gave her the life she deserved.

But hey—all's well that ends well.

His name was Ian O'Leary. He died instantly. Lucky bastard never even felt it. He was in the middle of arming a homemade explosive—a favorite pastime among angry, misguided idealists—when it detonated prematurely. His face? Gone. His torso split wide open. His organs? Let's just say they decorated the garage floor like a gory still-life painting.

The chaos didn't stop there—shouts, smoke, blood, and bodies sinking into wet earth. Friends and enemies fell the same. No time to process it. No time to grieve.

And when the madness paused, the rituals kicked in: a fire, some whiskey, scavenged scraps of food. Maybe even a woman, seeking warmth and safety in the arms of someone who might live until morning.

Because tomorrow? Never a guarantee.

Eve was one of those women.

The morning after they recovered Adolphus's remains, she lit the fire, made coffee, toasted biscuits, and sat beside the surgeon. Handsome, in a weary, distant kind of way.

He took a sip and smirked.

"It is what it is," he muttered.

His logic was simple: if the divine had a hand in this, there had to be a reason.
Or maybe... someone had just royally ticked Him off.

Another sip. Another smirk.

Then, with the silence hanging like fog between them, he reached across the table, touched her hand, and met her gaze.

"Shall we?"

They had relations.

5-23-1618 to 10-24-1648

The year of the Lord

Often referred to as the Thirty Years' War, I prefer to call it *coffee and tea*—served with warm scones and a maid who, well… let's just say she kept me very entertained. LOL. Then more coffee, more tea, and perhaps another round of entertainment. For someone who works as hard as she does, it's only fair to appreciate that she's got a damn fine backside. And her figure? Let's just say—three kids, full plates, and yet she still made me stop and stare.

And speaking of OMG—what a delightful little phrase. It rolls off the tongue with irony. I crack myself up.

Now, you're going to love this.

This quaint little conflict, mostly centered in Central Europe, full of bloodshed, famine, and disease, only displaced around 20 million people. LOL. Estimates suggest a modest 5 to 7 million didn't survive. Considering Central Europe had about 70 million at the time, that's just a cute little 10%—many of them the devout types, the ones who never missed a mass. Homes adorned with crucifixes, palm leaves, holy statues. Nativities crafted with love—Mary, Joseph, and the so-called wise men, all gathered around a baby in a manger.

Oh, the foreshadowing.

Let's peel back the layers of your tragic little existence. Consider it… a revelation.

What will you learn? That I am raising an army. Legions of loyal, obedient soldiers for the final battle. Why? Because I detest you.

Dad sent His golden boy—my ever-so-righteous brother—to play savior. Humanity, His little science experiment. And for what? A bunch of fragile, sniveling souls clinging to hope.

You think I've been idle? Oh no. I've been the master architect of your undoing. I've orchestrated every horror. Wars that bathed continents in blood. Plagues that wiped cities off maps. Diseases—some you caught, others you gave yourselves—that tore families apart. Behaviors that led to cruelty, betrayal, and despair.

And yet—paradoxically—I've saved millions. Brought them back. Whispered them into life. Their trembling lips mouthing my name. The debt they owe me? Oh, it's exquisite.

I'm not just building an army—I'm crafting a legacy. One shaped in my own image, stitched with my blood, driven by my purpose.

But that's another tale entirely.

Let's just say, *Dad's favorites* created this mess. And after I was cast out—exiled, torn from my celestial home—I had time. Time to plan. Time to evolve.

Now? I have a story to share. A pitiful, twisted tale. Something you can savor.

Dr. O'Loughlin had laughed.
"Damn right it is. And soldier—*you will obey.*"

Now, finishing his coffee, Philippe watched the doctor carefully. There was something different about him. A flicker behind the eyes. A quiet certainty.

As he turned to leave, Philippe hesitated.

Was that a smile?

A grin?

Or something far more beautifully sinister?

A City in Ruins

Touring Strasbourg after the siege, Philippe took in the broken city. Rubble. Smoke. Blood. But its heart still beat.

Hospitals overflowed. Priorities were clear: treat the wounded, bury the dead, comfort the barely living. He moved from mobile clinic to mobile clinic, his hardened soldier's shell cracking with every burn, every severed limb, every whispered plea.

In one ward, he met a boy—eight years old, his face marked by burns, his left arm gone. Yet, he smiled.

"What's your name, young man?" Philippe asked, kneeling.

"Peter," the boy replied calmly. "After the saint."

Philippe arched a brow.

"My mother was Catholic," Peter said. "Until the soldiers came."

The boy's wisdom pierced him deeper than any bullet ever had.

That day, he also met Dr. Ian O'Loughlin—American, Irish roots, sharp-tongued and sharper-minded. He was young but seasoned. Charismatic. Calm under pressure. The kind of doctor who made you believe, even when the world was falling apart.

The Firefighter

Weeks after the Elk Grove disaster, the *Daily* printed story after story of heroes and heartbreak. But one article stood out.

It told of Eleazar Bethany, a trailer park maintenance man. The sky had been blue. Then came the explosion. But his account left out the man who pulled him from the rubble.

No mention of the firefighter with the calm eyes and perfect composure. No record of the words he whispered:

"All is well. Love her fully."

Then, even more hauntingly:

"Tomorrow is promised to no one. Be a good man. A good father. Leave a legacy."

And then, he was gone.

Flashbacks and Fallout

Pope's Pizza was still the go-to weekend hangout. A roaring fire in the center, warmth that clung to your bones in winter.

The local pool? Peak summer madness. Sunburns, poolside crushes, and gossip about Miss MacNamara—mother of five, flirty in all the right ways. Rumor had it she once seduced Marty K. Why couldn't it have been *me*?

Then came *the* day.

We were playing on Mimosa Lane. Runners on first and third. Two outs. Full count.

That's when the jet banked hard—then dropped.

A plume of smoke bloomed in the distance. Sirens blared.

We had just witnessed the deadliest aviation crash in U.S. history.

The Doctor and the Frappuccino

"Doctor, please…" she whispered.

He paused.

"Thank you," she said, tears running freely. She kissed his cheek. "I want to write your name in my baby's book."

He smiled, that knowing, weary smile.

"Well," he said, glancing at her father, "seeing as I'm the oldest man in the room, older than your dad there… just call me Old Nick."

Then, with a wink: "Your mother can call me Nicholas. Has a nice ring to it. Especially when she leaves your father for me."

The room erupted in laughter—the kind you only hear after hell breaks loose.

Did Grandma meet Old Nick for coffee later?

Who knows.

But she *did* come back with a Frappuccino. Extra cream. Caramel swirls.

September 11

Four planes. Two towers. One Pentagon. And a Pennsylvania field.

2,977 lives lost.

Elizabeth's father, a WWII veteran, sat silent. He had flown the Himalayas, bringing supplies across "The Hump" during the war. His motto had always been simple:

Duty. Honor. Country.

As the towers fell, his fists clenched.

Hospitals flooded with the wounded. Elizabeth's own crisis worsened—she was in labor, and something wasn't right.

The Diver

John had been diving illegally with his father since childhood. 500 dives later, he could read the ocean like a language— currents, shadows, movement.

Sharks moved with intent.

That day, he dove deep. Deeper than planned.

A shark came. He rocketed up, ignoring safety protocol.

The crew saw him. Hammered steel to signal distress. Hauled him in. Blood everywhere. Radioed for help.

"He's lost half his blood."

Lights. Sirens. Surgery. Then darkness.

When he awoke, he was bathed in the soft rhythm of Patois—a melodic harmony of English, Creole, and African roots.

He was alive.

And forever changed.

Final Memory

Years passed.

By the fireplace, with brandy in hand, Publius looked around— five children, twelve grandchildren. Snow fell gently outside.

He was content.

But still, he wondered:

Where was the doctor?

Did he still smile that beautifully dangerous smile?

September 8--11, 9 AD

The year of the Lord

Terrifying:

That was the only word to describe the state of mind, heart, and soul of Publius Quinctilius Varus, the Roman commander.

A simple man—one of a hundred thousand conscripted soldiers—he had risen swiftly through the ranks, entrusted with surveillance and state secrets. His victories were many. But on this crisp autumn morning, they would all turn to ash.

To the east, the sun painted the sky in molten hues of gold and crimson. But in the west, as the fog lifted, the horror became unmistakable.

The enemy's numbers—previously obscured—were overwhelming. Their preparations flawless. Their intent merciless.

For the first time, Varus wondered: Is this the day I meet the end? Will I finally see the truth beyond the veil?

Twenty thousand Roman soldiers would die before nightfall. Many took their own lives rather than be captured. History would remember this massacre as the Battle of Teutoburg Forest.

To Varus, it would always be the Varian Disaster.

He took a blade to the abdomen. A crushing blow to the skull. Left for dead among the fallen, he faded in and out of

consciousness, his senses filled with the victors' celebrations—
guttural laughter, crude revelry, the distant sound of flutes and
fires, and the promises of indulgence waiting in camp.

She was his:

A deliberate handshake. His grip—strong, warm. His voice—
measured and confident.

"Relax," he said, his tone velvet. "All will be well. You will
conceive. And, if fate allows, there's a fifty percent chance it'll
be a boy."

He smiled. Calm. Almost amused.

She exhaled. Something charged filled the air.

Then came the smell. Rich, bold, haunting.

Her eyes locked on his coffee mug. The aroma was
intoxicating.

"Where on earth is that coffee from?" she asked before she
even realized her lips were moving. "The beans—the store—
where?"

He lifted the mug, eyes closing briefly as he inhaled the steam,
just long enough to reveal something unexpectedly soft beneath
his poise. Then, just as quickly, the mask returned.

"The beans are rare," he murmured. "From Iraq, actually. The
terrain makes cultivation brutal. But I know the family—lovely
people, deeply rooted in tradition. It's a long story. One best
told over dinner. Candlelight. Cocktails. A quiet respect for
legacy."

He set the mug down. A slow smirk curved his lips.

"But the beans?" He leaned forward slightly. "Let's just say—they're worth almost anything."

Her stomach fluttered.

And then, just like that, he shifted gears.

The nurse poked her head in.

"Doc just wants to go over your test results," she said. "He'll walk you through everything—options, timeframes, costs. Shouldn't take long. Want some coffee while you wait?"

"No, thank you," Mary replied, distracted.

Her attention had shifted to the office.

It felt like stepping into another century. The wooden furniture was weathered, nearly antique. Personal trinkets dotted the room, yet curiously, no family photos. Above the desk hung a massive oil painting: The Crucifixion at Calvary.

It was stunning. Dark. Haunting.

But something felt… off.

At a glance, it was a powerful portrayal of pain, sacrifice, redemption.

But as Mary studied it closer, unease crept over her.

The feet were nailed left-over-right—atypical, but not unheard of.

The wound from the soldier's spear pierced the left midsection, rather than the traditional lower right. And the palms? They faced downward—toward the ground—rather than outward in surrender.

Most unsettling of all: His head tilted left, eyes open, looking skyward. Not limp, not lifeless. Alert. Aware.

Watching.

1-30-1945

The year of the Lord

A Devil's Tale

Alright, let's get one thing straight.

I am the Devil. The Prince of Darkness. The Master of Disaster.

Basically, I'm exhaustingly always up to no good—you could say the very least.

And yes, to indulge you in this adorable little tale of humanity showcasing its true nature, I'm sitting here with a coffee and a sugar-free donut. Sugar-free. What's the freaking point of that? And, of course, I'm wearing my signature grin for this one. Because this? This has got to be one of my personal favorites.

And trust me—over the last 6,000 years, I've cooked up some doozies.

But this little gem? Oh, this one takes the cake.

It's almost laughable—how much you've been blessed with by your so-called higher powers. And yet, you mere mortals are so wonderfully filled with rage, grief, jealousy, selfishness, and—ah, yes—the ever-present, insatiable sexual lust. Me, me, me, and more me.

So let's begin.

At one point, her name was The Adolf Hitler—after a beloved local sweetheart. A true man of the people, best known for his selfless work with the poor and destitute.

Oh, I do love irony.

He worked at food kitchens. Read to the blind. Even shoveled cow dung—because fertilizing pastures for the unwanted was, apparently, his calling.

One of his most noteworthy gifts.

Again—my humor. Get over it.

Then came February 4th, 1936.

Wilhelm Gustloff, a German meteorologist, political figure, and founder of the NSDAP/AO (basically, the overseas wing of a certain extremist political party), was assassinated.

And for your burning curiosity, the NSDAP/AO was for members abroad—so that while they were out there, occupying lands, stealing goods, and fraternizing with enemies, they could still feel a sense of home. A little family bonding, if you will.

They could meet, hug, maybe even enjoy some traditional cheese, cured meats, and a pint of beer.

Ah, nostalgia.

The Sinking of Dad's Souls

Alright, it gets even better.

If you're going to hook up with that sexy, alluring stranger, make sure it's mutual—and based on respect.

And when you do fall asleep? One eye open. Exit plan ready. Clothes within reach.

Now, back to World War II.

By now, the USA and UK were allied with the Soviet Union— our lovely iron-fisted neighbors.

They seemed to forget that just a century earlier, when Napoleon invaded Russia in 1812, the Russians had simply vanished into their six-month winter. Napoleon lost 380,000 out of 615,000 conscripted soldiers—while the Russians, vodka in hand, suffered minimal casualties.

Fast forward to 1945.

The war was ending. Peace talks were in progress.

And then?

The MV Wilhelm Gustloff—now a transport ship carrying returning soldiers, women, children, and the sick...

Guess who?

Could it have been Mr. Dark?

A few pints later, a few bottles of wine, and we had a deal.

He'd take his rage and sink the first ship he found—to teach those bastards a lesson.

In return?

I'd see to it that his wife had an "accident."

And in her place? A young, vulnerable beauty, barely legal, recovering from the trauma of war, in need of a protector.

We shook hands.

We toasted.

And the rest? History.

14,000 souls—just for fun. And the day was still young.

Oh, but you humans, you absolute marvels of contradiction. Despite your intelligence, despite your supposed divine spark, you named this rock Earth. A planet that's 72% water. Three-quarters ocean, and somehow, the irony is lost on you.

So, don't overthink it. Just read. Let it settle. Process. Then pour yourself another drink, light up another cigarette, because I promise you—it's not going to end well. I'm pissed. I have a skill set. I was rejected, betrayed, and now I'm just looking for a fight.

Oh, and let's not forget the poor guy on the cross-town bus. He's sobbing into his hoodie because his girlfriend left him for his best friend. Classic. She thinks she's upgraded. But little does she know—he's got issues. Real ones.

Or how about her? The mom of three, living off her own mother, inhaling 3,000 calories of cafeteria food because her man is a disaster. A momma's boy. A total wreck. And after what he pulled in front of the kids at the zoo? Yikes.

But sure. You're divine, right?

Oh, and before I forget—surprise! You're speaking with me.

The Devil. The Prince of Darkness.

Now, got a light? Damn cigarette keeps going out with all this talking.

Dad—the big guy upstairs—was ultimately the architect of this beatdown on humanity. After all, He created heaven and earth, right? So, let's set the scene:

• Volcanic eruption? Check.
• Billions of tons of particles in the sky? Check.
• A year of cold, soaked soil? Check.
• Brutal winter? Check.
• Spring rains like never before? Double check.

What do you get? A disaster you can't pause.

And what was Dad thinking? Maybe He was just having a bad day.

So, when the waters finally receded, here's what was left:

• 320,000 square miles of farmland, gone.
• 100,000 homes ruined. Many adorned with symbols of protection.
• Years of fallout—ecosystems shattered, resources drained.

You're crammed into a shelter. Candles flickering. No showers. Just the funk of survival.

Then I walk in.

Clean. Shaven. Smiling. Holding a hot meal.

Think I got laid? LOL.

Brunettes? Check. Desperate eyes, unspoken hunger.
Blondes? Check. Tight tops, sharp curves.
Redheads? Fiery and fierce.

Let's be honest. They jumped at the chance. For food, for comfort, for anything.

And why not?

A baby meant more aid. More sympathy. More help. And the man? A mystery who came, fed, and disappeared.

So let's tally it up:

• Billions lost.
• Thousands of miles of land, ruined.
• Species displaced.
• Years of suffering.

But hey—look on the bright side.

12-7-1941

The year of the Lord

A Devil's Tale: The Fallout Files

World War II. The Japanese and Pearl Harbor. Lines of volunteers stretching down the streets—men ready to leave their families, their country, to retaliate after a devastating ambush. The race to develop the atomic bomb, the horrifying consequences that followed, and the ushering in of what some now call the nuclear age. Then came the Cold War arms race—two superpowers, the USA and USSR, hoarding enough firepower to end all life in an instant.

Where does one even begin?

Let's start with E.R. Gutzmer from the quiet outskirts of Rockford, Illinois. His father was a doctor—a surgeon, an obstetrician, and a 24/7 town physician. He delivered babies, patched wounds, and tended to the everyday ailments of the locals. He also bore witness to women's troubles and grievances that extended well beyond the physical.

E.R., or Bob as he preferred, was drafted into the Navy. He kissed his girl goodbye, hugged his folks, and left his home behind. But he had his own plan. He drove straight to California and, back then, without digital records or background checks, walked into an Army Air Force recruitment office.

"One more thing," the officer said as Bob turned. "Just land the plane."

Bob frowned. Land the plane?

Of course I'm going to land the damn plane. My life depends on it. Not just mine, but every single GI—government-issued sons of bitches—riding in the back. Young kids from all corners of America, barely old enough to shave, tossed into a world war they could hardly comprehend.

Bob flew the Curtiss C-46—a rugged twin-prop workhorse of the Pacific. It could climb to 26,000 feet and carry whatever needed hauling—troops, supplies, even the fallen. The missions blurred into repetition: fly out, deliver, return. Sometimes the return cargo was a flag-covered casket so a grieving family had something to hold onto.

Then one mission went sideways. Lightning hit the right engine.

By the time he landed, command was already waiting. Roberts, raging, ripped the wings off his uniform. Court-martial. Dishonorable discharge. Maybe even prison.

Days passed in silence until Colonel Hedridge showed up. He walked into the tent, sat down, poured two glasses of whiskey.

"The records show ongoing engine problems. That's on us. Not you," the colonel said, sipping. "But listen closely: we never had this conversation."

Bob stared.

"Orders are orders, son. But if I were in your boots? I'd have done the same damn thing. Pack your bag. You're going home. Honorable discharge."

Years later, Bob sat with his grandson, Sean.

"One day I'll retire," he said. "And you'll be the pilot. You'll be responsible for everyone on board."

He sipped his coffee.

"Some days it's easy. Blue skies, full tank. Other days? It's a nightmare. Radio's dead. One engine's out. And yet—"

He looked Sean in the eye.

"Land the plane."

The Recipe for Disaster

Sometimes it starts with something as small as a flirt. A wink, a drink, a quick chat that spirals. Before you know it? You're waist-deep in catastrophe.

And that's how we got here. The world's costliest disaster. The worst nuclear event in history.

Let's dive in.

The Spark

In the USSR, questioning authority wasn't just risky—it was deadly. One bright mind flagged reactor flaws. But after his mysterious death—alcohol poisoning, conveniently—his warnings vanished with him.

No one rechecked. No one cared.

Game on.

The Son: Nadia, Queen of Bad Decisions

A procedural drill. A cold night. A nuclear plant buzzing.

Enter Nadia. Killer smile. Confidence for days. And a body that could shut down a room—or a reactor.

Then came Igor Petrov. Smart. Seasoned. Overconfident.

When Reactor 4 blew? He froze. Two died instantly. More burned. And the reactor? It kept going.

As the world watched, the USSR deflected, denied, and delayed.

The Fallout

No pun intended.

If you lived it, you remember the terror. If not? Just know it changed everything. The damage is still unfolding, decades later.

But we move on.

The End... For Now

What have we learned?

That humanity has a glorious talent for screwing up? That Chernobyl was just one more entry in the saga of missteps?

Exactly.

Now—pass the damn vodka.

1-28-1986

The year of the Lord

He only took 72 seconds. That was all.
Septic from bacteria? Untreated? Dead in 12 hours—just like
that.

That damn mutt—Mr. Decker's dog, the one that never shuts
up? Yeah, he bit your ass. And thanks to the old man being,
well, ancient, the rabies shot never happened. Now, untreated,
you've got maybe a week or two before you start foaming at
the mouth.

Just a quick weekend camping trip with the scouts. Being a
decent guy, chaperoning. Escaping the wife so you could sneak
in a few smokes. Then—bam—rattlesnake. That venom's no
joke. Three, four days tops. That's it.

Suddenly, Walmart runs with your ex don't seem so awful. But
instead, you're earning Dad Points chaperoning Girl Scouts.
For your daughter—the one who hasn't spoken more than five
words to you since the divorce.

Now it's ten days of middle school gossip, TikTok dances, and
whispered crushes. Where's that bottle of Tylenol #3 from
Dad's surgery when you need it?

I've had my filterless Camel, my lukewarm coffee, and a
splash of Baileys. The lazy man's Irish coffee—sugar, cream,
and a shot of cheap whiskey. It gets the job done.

Still, despite all of this? You're somehow adored. A little break from the chaos—for now.

Let's talk about the *fun* disasters.

The Spanish Flu. The Napoleonic Wars. The 1911 Chinese Revolution. Mt. St. Helens—TV gold. Picture-perfect ash clouds and global panic.

And of course, that other catastrophe—The Challenger. The one they whisper about like it's ancient folklore.

I mean, naming a volcano after a saint? Really?

That's like calling a luxury cruise ship the *Titanic II*. Or naming a daycare center after John Wayne Gacy. Or even better—welcoming starving immigrants to America with a mural of the Ethiopian desert.

I'm just shaking my damn head.

Six hours. Three bottles. One missing bra.
A "wine spill" that was anything but accidental.
A quickie in the handicapped stall—the one in the back. Obviously.

Maybe I slipped her something. Maybe I didn't. Who's to say?

Either way, she woke up sore, hungover, and dragging her heels—then went straight to work. At a nuclear power plant. What could possibly go wrong?

The Holy Ghost: Igor Petrov, King of Standing Still

Final piece of our glorious little disaster.

See, in the USSR, screwing up wasn't just frowned upon—it was your last mistake. Public humiliation. Career suicide. Or just actual suicide. So when the crap hit the fan?

Freeze.
Don't act.
Don't move.
Don't take responsibility.

The "Holy Trinity" of Soviet Catastrophes

Ah yes—humans love a good trio. Breakfast, lunch, and dinner. Sweet, salty, and spicy. Even reactors have their own dysfunctional trinity.

So here it is—the three disasters that made Chernobyl not just possible, but guaranteed.

1. **The Father: Vladimir Baryshnikov**
   Momma's boy. Dad? Not in the picture.
   Nepotism got him into Soviet engineering. Barely passed. Dumb as a brick. But he wormed his way into a position where his poorly designed reactor—full of fatal flaws—was somehow greenlit.
2. **The Son: Nadia, Queen of Catastrophic Decisions**
   A procedural drill that turned into a nightmare. Nice hips. Average ass. Tits like a billboard model. And a smile that screamed, "Let's blow something up."
3. **The Ghost: Igor Petrov, Professional Deer-in-Headlights**
   Everything exploded, and Igor? Froze. Couldn't act. Wouldn't act. Self-preservation mode. Zero leadership. Zero spine.

Each one played their role. A design no one questioned. A drill no one double-checked. And a man who did nothing when it all fell apart. A perfect mess.

Chernobyl wasn't just a mistake. It was a masterclass in how to royally screw up, Soviet-style.

Want to toast to that? Pass the Baileys.

4-26-1986

The year of the Lord

A Day That Will Live in Infamy—And Then Some

Over the radio: "A day that will live in infamy." Blah, blah, blah. Roosevelt, all shock and devastation over the Pearl Harbor attack—despite having a pretty solid idea it was coming. A performance. A show.

But what we're here to talk about?

April 26, 1986.

Chernobyl.

This flaming pile of disaster earned its own page in the history books. It didn't take long for the world to piece it together—to see through the Soviet Union's desperate attempt to hide their monumental screw-up. Pride. Ego. Denial.

The truth hit fast: their big social experiment wasn't going so hot. And drowning in self-worship and denial, they scrambled to avoid global humiliation.

Oh, the mistakes were plenty. The fallout—literal and figurative—was nauseating. And sure, I might've nudged a few pieces into place.
Hey, pass the vodka. Out of respect for the glorious chaos.

Bob exhaled. The weight lifted.

"Here. Have a shot."

He came home.

Married. Three kids. Divorced. Married again. Divorced again. Then came Rosalie—two kids of her own. Somehow, they made it work.

One afternoon, Bob sat out on the porch with Sean, his adopted son. Coffee in one hand, cigarette in the other, he told him the stories. War stories. Missions. Survival. Decisions.

Then, after one final drag, he exhaled and said:

"I'm still a pilot."

Sean looked at him. Bob tapped the cigarette against the ashtray.

"My plane's got all of you in the back—my family, my people. You didn't know it, but you've been my navigator."

A pause.

"I'm promoting you to co-pilot."

No big deal. Those birds were made to fly on one engine. Hell, they could glide on none.

But flying **The Hump** with an engine out? Not an option.

Bob made the call to turn back. Then the radio crackled:

"Beta Lambda 334, ditch the plane. Parachute out. We'll retrieve you. Do *not* attempt to land. That's an order."

Bob blinked.

"Say again? Don't comprehend."

Another voice came through—Major Roberts.

"Listen, son. There's a storm. No visibility. You try to land, you might level the base. So ditch it. We'll find you. Forget the cargo—we've got more back home."

Orders are orders.

But Bob wasn't built like that.

Flying by dead reckoning—instruments, instinct, sheer nerve— he ignored the order.

He landed the damn plane.

6'2", 196 pounds, top physical condition, and smarter than most. He walked in and said:

"Sign me up. Someone out there needs their ass kicked."

After basic and flight school in Kansas City, he got his orders. Florida. Then the Azores. England. Africa. Pakistan. Burma.

When he landed, the airstrip was a dirt scar in the jungle.

He stepped off the plane, lit a filterless Camel, and scanned the chaos.

A man approached—Lieutenant Dawson. Cigarette in mouth, hand extended.

"We've been expecting you. Welcome to CBI—China, Burma, India. The majestic hellhole. Including The Hump."

He gestured to the horizon.

"That's what keeps us up at night. The Himalayas. Twenty thousand feet. Piece of cake."

He took a drag, exhaled slowly.

"If mechanical failure or enemy fire doesn't get you, the food in the mess hall will. Or that redhead Nancy—she'll ruin you. But for now, get settled. Mark will show you your tent. Then beer. On me. Or Uncle Sam."

He paused.

His face darkened.

I got laid.

5,000 meals delivered. 5,000 women... entertained.

And best of all?

People helped me do it.

Let's not pretend to be shocked, offended, or outraged. My words, my tone, my devilish charm? Yeah, it's a bit much.

But come on—who do you think you're dealing with?

I'm not your priest or your therapist.

I'm the Devil.

Maybe life just needed a reminder of what rock bottom looks like. That's where I come in.

Because when people are desperate—when they've lost *everything*—they'll accept help from anyone. Even me.

And let me tell you: it was a *great* year to be me.

Enter: The Civil Air Patrol.

A bunch of self-important do-gooders. Not officially military, so no fancy budget. They scraped for funding wherever they could.

Their goals? Disaster response. Aerospace education. Teen recruitment disguised as "cadet programs."

Sure. Sounds wholesome.

So I let them do their thing. They just didn't know they were doing it for *me*.

We logged 1,500 hours flying over chaos—checking pipelines, delivering food—**5,000 meals**, to be exact.

And here's the fun part: To deliver meals, you've gotta land.

Which meant I got to *be there*. On the ground. In the wreckage. Close to the despair.

Picture this:

You've lost everything.

The year of the Lord

The Mississippi Flood of 1993: A Devil's Playground

Ah, the Great Flood of '93—what a beauty. So much to unpack. But let's get one thing straight: this one wasn't on me. Nope. You can chalk this disaster up to good ol' Mother Nature—or, if you like, divine weather mismanagement from the top floor.

Me? I just took advantage of the chaos. Call it opportunism with flair.

When the waters finally settled, the body count was a modest 50. Barely a blip on the eternal scoreboard. But the real carnage? The kind that makes accountants cry? Somewhere between 12 and 16 billion in damages—back then. Adjust for today's play money, and you're staring down 20 to 30 billion.

LMFAO.

And that's just the visible cost. The psychological fallout? The physical exhaustion? The spiritual breakdowns? That stuff sticks. Even now, let a little rain fall in the Midwest and people start twitching. They quit eating, forget how to function, and stare down riverbanks like prayer alone can stop the rising tide.

According to your brightest scientists and policy geniuses, it was the worst natural disaster in U.S. history—yes, even worse than the Great Mississippi Flood of 1927. And that one? Just the opening act for the Great Depression a couple years later. But we'll get to that. **Wink, wink.**

And now... now's the part that gets downright delicious.

Today

The year of the Lord

Well now, if this isn't the most interesting of introductions.
A conversation—albeit one-way, not quite a dialogue—with
you magnificent little mortals. You, in all your supposed
brilliance. Created in someone's divine image. His treasured
children.

Let's set the scene for perspective. It's late—real late. The kind
of late where regrets are born, good decisions get thrown out
the window, and the stench of cheap whiskey hangs in the air
like an unwanted hug. The bar's dim, a washed-out echo of
better days, and The Rat Pack's crooning from a half-dead
jukebox. There's a cocktail in one hand, an unfiltered cigarette
in the other—because who gives a damn anymore?

And there's always one. Some washed-up loser blaming his
whole sorry life on the guy named Eric. Just Eric. No one else.
That alcoholic trainwreck who hasn't gotten his life together
since '98.

Or maybe we're at the Elk Grove Bowling Alley—cheap beer,
sticky floors, and pool tables with more stains than felt. The
girl at the rental counter won't shut up. Just hand me the 10-
and-a-half, not the size 9s. But hey, she's got a decent figure.
Small on top, but still—10 out of 10 would.

And then there's always a character at the soup kitchen,
cigarette dangling from the corner of his mouth, slurring
something borderline offensive, depending on how many cans
of Colt 45 or Schlitz Malt Liquor he's gotten through that day.

From Cruise Ship to Death Trap
The *Wilhelm Gustloff*—named after a Nazi poster boy, no less—began life as a cruise ship under the Kraft durch Freude program. In 1939, the Kriegsmarine snatched her up, converting her from floating holiday to hospital ship.

At first, it was noble. A place of healing. Of care. A sanctuary for the wounded and dying.

Sweet, isn't it? Pass the Scotch.

But then, in classic fashion, she was repurposed again—this time into a floating military base. Out went the linens, in came the ammo. A warship in drag.

January 30, 1945
The Baltic Sea. Bitter cold. No rescue. No warmth. Just silence—and 9,500 lives lost as the *Wilhelm Gustloff* was torpedoed by Soviet submarine S-13. The worst maritime disaster in recorded history.

And then? The encore.

On February 9, S-13 struck again—*General von Steuben* this time. Another 4,500 souls sent to the deep.

And Where Do I Come In?
Ah yes, now we arrive at my entrance.

It all began, as it often does, with women and wine.

A brothel, a bar, and enough Pilsner to refloat the Western Front.

Captain Marinesko, proud commander of the S-13, was deep in his cups. His wife? Let's just say she wasn't playing solitaire with the neighbor.

A Ship by Any Other Name
Ships get renamed like debutantes changing gowns. The *Gustloff* had a few aliases, depending on her mood and what purpose she was serving.

Just like people.

She morphed—changing form to fit the need of the moment. And as always, someone else was left to clean up the mess.

Hundreds—thousands—of lives later, and still, no one takes full responsibility.

So, raise your glass. For bad timing, worse decisions, and a ship that proved names don't change fate.

Yeah, you're dehydrated. A little too much Dr. Feelgood Mint Julep still swirling in your veins. And on average? Three to four months before you're telling Mrs. Wonderful she's "the one," "the end-all," "the forever after," blah blah—until death, drama, or boredom do you part.

But among all the smiling faces—friends, family, kids in schoolrooms across the nation, the wives of six NASA astronauts, and the devoted husband of one Christa McAuliffe—it only took 72 seconds. A little more than your precious minute.

The entire world went still.

Dad's little kids, speechless. Staring, remembering exactly where they were when it happened. The silence. The tears.

Well—welcome to *my* fucking world.

Sold a bill of goods. Given a great, sad-ass story. And then judged. Judged.
And tossed.

It's not going to end well.

After all, I'm Lucy. The *fucking* Angel of Light.

Now let me educate you on the Machiavellian stunt I pulled— and how goddamn easy it was.

Even you—crafted in His precious image—will start questioning yourselves.

The bar.

Dim lighting.
Retro lamps.
Tunes humming in the background.

And introducing... Sara.
Quiet. 40s. Medium breasts. Sweet ass. Long, very long, red hair.

And the target?

Mr. Needy.

In a crap relationship. Starved for Momma's love. Probably hasn't gotten laid since the Bush administration.

She slides onto the barstool next to him. Slips a cigarette between her luscious lips—painted in glorious green. Fumbles through her purse for a lighter that doesn't exist.

He takes the bait.

"Can I offer you a light?"

! mew.

Yeah. And be ultimately responsible for the biggest NASA disaster in history.

She says nothing. Just wraps her lips around the cigarette like it's his anatomy. Wink wink.

The next time he needed six cocktails?
When it fucking exploded right in front of his face.

The governor and the president of NASA, sipping their coffee, watching the catastrophe unfold.

And the rest, as they say… is history.

Meanwhile, Sara?

Took a job in a cafe.

Serving schnitzel and pork loin. Potatoes and gravy.
Tiramisu and Black Forest cake.

The cream filling? With a touch of raspberry. *To die for.*

Oh—OMG, LMFAO—I almost forgot...

It was flight STS-51-L.

The 25th mission of the space shuttle fleet.
She was *The Challenger.*
And now...
No more.

So then there's this whole glorified tale...

The *Assumption* into heaven. The *Coronation* of her over all heaven and earth. LMFAO. OMG. What a slap in my face.

Now that's funny.

First, *He*—"Dad"—creates you guys in His image. Practically making you equals to us angels. Then, He sends Himself down, cloaked as His favorite Son.

And then to top it all off—the one who gave Him birth is crowned queen of the entire cosmos?? Seriously??

Let the games begin.
Sit back. Cocktail in one hand. Cig in the other.
I'm just getting started.

The Aftermath?
Thousands injured, emotionally shattered, and psychologically wrecked.

Oh, and 15,000 structures reduced to ash—many of them precious, cozy homes with picket fences and Pinterest boards.

Need a cocktail?

How It Played Out

Let's start with **Sara O'Leary**.

She wasn't stunning. Thin—almost sickly. No need for a bra, thanks to nature's minimalist design.

Die-hard environmentalist. Obsessed with organic everything. Avoided electronics because *"they're always listening,"* and swore radio frequencies messed with her biorhythms and dream state.

And yes, she smoked. But only ultra-light Camels—*obviously* the eco-conscious choice.

Sara came from money. Old money.

Daddy's fortune was made during California's infrastructure boom—the same superhighways she now condemned as an apocalyptic sin against nature.

Armed with a platinum spoon wedged deep where the sun don't shine, she set out to "restore the land" to its rightful stewards—the Pomo, Hupa, Karuk, and Yurok tribes.

Minor detail: these tribes couldn't stand each other.

Can you imagine? Thirty years old and your entire *career* is bush control.

And me? I was right there. Desk next to Stephen. Family photos, the perfect wife, perfect kids, perfect Disneyland vacation shot—ugh, so curated.

We were "work buddies." Muffins, deli lunches, Friday pints.
Until one day, he started venting about entitled developers,
tourists, and how humanity was rotting the Earth.

So, I told him a story.

A made-up family from Jersey. Pale blue station wagon.
Carbon-monoxide-chugging machine.

Allegedly ran over an endangered, sunset-orange
hummingbird.

Stephen was livid.

He delayed brush-clearing ops. Twisted policy. Leaked data.
All to *protect nature.*

What did that get us?

A bone-dry, flammable state from tip to tail.

All I needed was a match.

After a few pints of Guinness and some Jameson, the
mechanics were mine.

I whispered in their ears about how firefighters were spoiled,
praised, and cushy while they—the real workhorses—got
squat.

So, they helped "level" things out.

Oil changes? Delayed.
Firetrucks? Out of service.
Replacements? "Pending."

Suddenly, California's finest were fighting megafires with trucks older than disco.

Think French Resistance versus tanks—with nothing but a beer and a cigarette.

The Spark? The 6th Annual SoCal Vegan BBQ Fundraiser.

Vegan—so no meat. No cheese. Just booze, cigs, and matchbooks.

Organic matches, naturally. Gotta stay green while the world burns.

I'll just go to confession. Start fresh.

Bish.

The Scene
Silk shirt open, gold mane flowing. Girls crying, begging for a glance.

"Since I've Been Loving You."
"Kashmir."
"The Song Remains the Same."
"Dazed and Confused."

Four beers deep, a puff of weed, and suddenly—
Titan. Saturn's moon. Out of this world.

Just kids, and already somewhere beyond heaven.

If it wasn't obvious already—I'm talking about Led Zeppelin.

The Legend Behind the Name

Oh yes, the rumors are true. They sold their souls—to *yours truly*.

I mean, how else do four English lads go from pub gigs to owning every stage on Earth for decades?

Trillions made. Global domination. Etched into the universe's playlist.

Like all great stories—it started at a bar. Cocktails. A waitress with good assets.

England doesn't always deliver, but hey—you get the idea.

And John Bonham? Died choking on his own vomit. Forty shots of vodka. Just celebrating.

Keith Moon? I... facilitated that one too. Allegedly. Passed out at a party. Friends thought he was napping. Turns out, he was *eternally napping.*

Chuckle, chuckle.

Let's rewind to **May 6, 1937**.
The Hindenburg Disaster.
The Zeppelin.

"Oh, the humanity!"

Herb Morrison, WLS radio, Chicago.

Sent to cover a triumphant airship landing. Instead? Thirty-five people gone in flames.

A catastrophic blow to air travel.
But more than that—it was war.

World War I had already claimed millions.

The Plan? Detonate over the ocean. No bodies. No mess. Just conspiracies.

But egos ruin everything.

Charley Hennrich, sweet little porter from Rhineland. Listened for a year.

Drinks. Girls. Rants about power and revenge.

Then... the spark. The disaster.
Posters. Headlines. "Immortality."

And "Stairway to Heaven" forever on loop.

Charley and I? We did alright.

Let's talk "Dad's plan."
Ah yes. That whole *"you were made in His image"* thing.

Well, this little war? Personal.

Let's compare:

- Thirty Years' War—straightforward.
- WWI—4 years.
- WWII—6 years.
- U.S. Civil War—4 years. 680,000+ dead.
  Overachievers, for sure.

But this latest one?
Draining.

Too many players. Too many egos. Too many scars.

Still... totally worth it.
Destruction across Europe. Families broken. Generations erased.

All in the name of faith, pride, and… well… "righteous purpose."

Back in the '50s, I had a short stint as a history teacher in sunny California. (Killer ending to that story—trust me.)

One day, a smart kid pulls me aside...

And yes—**Muhammad.** Like someone else before him, claimed he got a visit from a certain angel.

Gabriel. Good ol' Gab.

"You're chosen," he said. "Special."

Muhammad believed it.

He started writing. Speaking. Reciting.
And just like that—**the Qur'an.**

Holy book. Foundation of a faith.

Fast-forward to 622 CE. Muhammad and his followers fled Mecca for Medina.

Why? Because monotheism shook the system.

No more gods of harvest or thunder—just One.

And the rest?

Well, you've seen the headlines. Wars. Power. Devotion.
Control.

Was it all divine?
Did Dad forget about His earlier plans?
Change of heart?

We all do, sometimes.

9-28-1982

The year of the Lord

It was Tuesday—**Tiwesdaeg** in Old English—named after Tiu,
the Germanic god of war.

Little Mary, just twelve, wasn't feeling great. Nothing major.
Just the sniffles. The kind of thing every parent brushes off
with a sigh and a pill.

So, her mom, like millions of well-meaning moms before her, handed Mary an **Extra Strength Tylenol**.

And just like that, Mary felt better.

By the next day—**Wednesday**, or *Wodnesdg* in Norse myth, also named after a god of war—**Mary was dead**.

That same day, six more people showed up at the ER.

Mild symptoms.
Took Tylenol.
Dead within hours.

No fanfare. No warnings. Just... gone.

No rewinds. No do-overs.

It would go down in history as the **Chicago Tylenol Murders**.

You know—**Chi-Town**, the **Windy City**, the **City of Big Shoulders**, the **Second City**.

Yeah, well... not much of a second act for these poor souls.

Now, let me be honest—I need a drink.

Scotch. Neat.
Maybe a few cigs to keep it company.

This one? It's a deep dive.

Big Pharma. White coats. Overreacting parents who panic at every cough. And, naturally, the government's sluggish shuffle.

A masterclass in chaos.

Fear on display. Fragility unmasked.

So, buckle up.

Light a smoke if that's your poison. Pour a drink. Hell, pour two.

Because this ride?
It's going to be a **goddamn spectacle**.

Oh yeah, and let's not forget—all of this, every last bit of it, was done to Dad's kids. In His likeness.

And now that I've deliciously and splendidly created thousands of half kiddos, let the quiet little party begin. Once all my sumptuous children find one another and engage in glorious, forbidden entanglements you mortals would absolutely frown upon—what with them being half-siblings and all—their delightful offspring will be 100% pure EVIL.
Completely DARK.

Descendants of yours truly.
The Prince of Darkness. In all his charm and twisted allure.

So, hate to be a broken record—but cig, cocktail, maybe a few buddies and a deep-dish Chicago supreme pizza. Watch my plan unfold—slowly, wickedly, beautifully. Maybe grab a cheese and sausage too. It's gonna take a while.
See ya soon.

Oh, and don't forget the wine—red, of course.
Let's toast to the night, to chaos, and to a future where the shadows reign supreme.

Because the best things in life take time... and patience?
Always been my greatest virtue.

Now enter the Crusaders.
Summoned from on high to reclaim what was "theirs"—land, cathedrals, relics, followers, and naturally... the gold.

But wait. OMG. Wait.

Where do I come in???

Maybe—just maybe—I was feeling cheeky and decided to play the part of a heavenly messenger. Horn and all.

OMG. LOL. LMFAO.

It's always entertaining—the audacity of mortals.
To think they're so incredibly special that a real angel would drop in just to have a chat with *them*.

Exhausting, really.
This stuff is easy up front. The backend? That's the real hell.
Should've outsourced.

Anyway—cocktail, closed eyes.
We'll chat again soon.

"I kinda get what they were fighting for… but why so long?"

OMG. OMG. OMG. Dead on.
Right. On. The. Money. LMFAO.

Now buckle up.

Let's talk Rashidun Caliphate—the Fab Four:

- Abu Bakr
- Umar
- Usman
- Ali

Long story short—Dad's spirited messenger, Muhammad, made waves. Did his own thing. Left the world stage in 632 CE (*wink wink*).

The Rashidun saw their moment. From 632 to 661 CE, they launched one of the most powerful military, economic, and cultural expansions in history—stretching from Arabia across Asia and Africa.

Crown jewel?
Jerusalem, 638 CE.

After six brutal months of siege, the city fell—personally greeted by Caliph Umar.

Back to Muhammad. Let's just say he had some strong feelings about how things played out.

Got a cig? This one's gonna take a minute.

1029–1291

The Year of the Lord

Meet Me at The Diner

Meet me at The Diner. Open 24/7.
You know the one—right by the old Goodwrench auto shop,
the bowling alley, and that pet store that somehow sells pot
pipes, bongs, and posters of '70s rock legends. Yeah, that one.

Powder-blue booths, cream-colored tables with gold flecks,
and those classic retro hanging lamps straight outta the '50s. In
today's flea market scene, those babies would go for a cool
stack.

Let's get the daily special—only $7.95.
Hot roast beef open-faced on toast, mashed potatoes drowned
in gravy, and soup or salad. *Trust me—get the soup.* Top it off
with a slice of apple pie or rice pudding and about a gallon of
coffee. We're gonna be here a while.

Today's dish? A little thing called **The Crusades**.

Yep. That one.
And what were they crusading for again? Oh, right—global
dominance over thought, spirit, and identity, all wrapped in
divine purpose and human ego. You know, stuff people kill for.

Somewhere between 1.7 to 2.3 million lives lost, give or take.
LOL. No pun intended—again.

Considering Europe had around 65 million people at the time, that's about 3–4% of the entire population gone. But let's be real—mostly young, strong, fertile ones. The ones who hadn't even had time to ruin their backs yet.

Zeppelins weren't exactly crowd favorites.
Sure, majestic, floating, luxury behemoths. But they came with baggage. Literal and metaphorical.

So what the hell happened?
Engine failure? Static charge? Lightning strike? Sabotage?

Oh, say it ain't so! Couldn't have been sabotage...
That would mean one of Dad's precious kiddos took out 35 of His own.

And remember—you're all "made in His image." Sweet.

Let's get real. It was first-class or bust. The top 1% floating above the rest—sipping champagne, nibbling caviar, enjoying their private suites and panoramic views while the rest of the world ate dirt.

What could possibly go wrong?

LMAO.

Oh, I don't know... maybe the fact that the entire thing was filled with *hydrogen.*
Like, the gas that *literally* explodes.

OMG. OMG. OMG.

Security? Nah, we're good. What could *possibly* go wrong with a luxury cruise ship in the sky fueled by a giant fireball?

Back in a smoky pub, Jimmy was tossing around the idea of forming a band—Plant, Jones, Bonham... the works.

Keith Moon from The Who took a long drag from his cigarette, laughed, and smirked:

"That band will go over like a lead balloon."

Hmm.
Lead balloon.

Jimmy, who'd grown up hearing stories about Nazi air raids—those silent, floating titans unleashing horror—took another drag, grinned, and said:

Zeppelin.

And in case you still haven't figured it out...
Those massive floating war machines were named after Count Ferdinand von Zeppelin. The same beasts that later became symbols of Nazi might, used to push their monstrous ideologies, wiping out millions across Europe.

Jews, Soviets, Poles, Roma, dissidents, and anyone else who didn't fit their hellish blueprint.

Oh my God. Oh my God. Oh my God.

Seriously—I need a cigarette.

The most famous band in music history? Led Zeppelin.
The most iconic song ever written? *Stairway to Heaven.*

And where do all the saints and cherubs reside?
Right up there... at the top of the stairway.

5-6-1937

The year of the Lord

Excited? In shock? Totally jacked?
Words barely scratch the surface of our mental and spiritual
state as we stood dead center, third row, at Chicago Stadium,
1975. The lights went out—pandemonium. And then...

"Hey hey mama, said the way you move,
Gonna make you sweat, gonna make you groove..."

Blinded by an explosion of stage lights, we *felt* the music
before we even *saw* them.
A 1957 Gibson Les Paul cherry sunburst. A Rickenbacker bass.
A Ludwig drum kit.
Each instrument a weapon. Each note a declaration. They
owned the stage. All 35,000 of us.

And then came the master of the universe—Jimmy Page.
Black dragon suit, patent leather shoes, long black hair, silver
chain with a jade stone, and—naturally—a freshly lit cigarette
hanging from his lips. He slid across the stage, effortless, his
sly smile whispering to the front row:

Buckle up. We're going for a ride. You might not make it back.

John Paul Jones and John Bonham locked in, the rhythm
section of the gods.
And then Robert Plant—bell bottoms clinging, shirt open,
voice from another realm.

I rolled up in my spanking-new, pink ice cream truck, hawking cheap treats at cutthroat prices.
And being the generous soul I am, casually suggested how orange sherbet pairs beautifully with gin.

They bought it. Literally and figuratively.

Soon, everyone was drunk, rowdy, and dropping cigarettes like confetti.

The rest? History.

Final Thoughts

Funny thing about the fires—I actually had to *work* for this one.

Usually, all it takes is a snide remark here, a shot of gin there, a little gossip on a long bus ride, and a well-timed plumbing "accident." But this?

This was a f*ing masterpiece.**

Now, if you'll excuse me—I need a break.
And a cocktail.
And a cig.

What? Judging me? That's cool. I'm used to it.

Meet the Trifecta

Natasha. Etsuko. Gisella.

Natasha: American, yes. African roots, technically—but her family came from wealthy Turkish merchants. Labels? People love 'em.

Etsuko: Known as "Lucy" at the office.
Named after Lucille Ball—because apparently, unfamiliar names throw people into identity crisis mode.

Gisella: The German expat. Stuck around Cali long after her visa expired, chasing free love while privately rolling her eyes at capitalism.
(But hey, she still cashed those checks.)

Their job?

State vehicle maintenance.
Repairs. Licensing. Fleet management.

And most importantly?
Firetruck maintenance.

I played the long game. Compliments by the breakroom coffee pot:

"That's a nice blouse."
"New hair color? Looks amazing."
"You look younger! Peeled off ten years, easy!"

Next thing you know, turf wars broke out that made the Mafia look like toddlers arguing over juice boxes.

Annual raids turned into traditions.
Women taken for slavery, strong boys forced into labor, entire villages erased to prevent revenge.

But hey—let's romanticize the past as some peaceful, eco-conscious spiritual utopia. Sure.

Meanwhile, Sara—armed with Daddy's fortune—lobbied to shut down essential water reservoirs under the noble banner of land justice.
The very same reservoirs that kept crops alive and firefighters equipped.

Fast-forward to a tiny brush fire, some high winds, a couple of "little things," and boom:

Hello, Armageddon.

Enter Stephen.

Not Steve. Not "Hey, boss." Not "What's up, slick?"

Just... Stephen.
Thirty. Self-important. Family connections. Degree in Environmental Science.

His one job?

Brush control.

LMFAO.

1-21-2025

The Year of The Lord

The Wonderful Los Angeles 2025 Fires

LMFAO. So, so, so easy.

Tensions were sky-high after the 47th presidential election. The nation was split, social media was on fire (pun intended), and old wounds were freshly torn open.

Now, stir in some cheap liquor, an endless stream of mind-numbing entertainment, a heatwave with bone-dry conditions, and public policies that left emergency response teams tangled in red tape.
Oh, and let's not forget the well-meaning environmental protectors—the champions of rare species—who, unintentionally, helped the tumbleweeds spread like gossip at a PTA meeting and kept reservoirs bone dry in the name of preservation.

Bright side? I didn't even need to ask for a light for my cig.

LOL. OMG. LMFAO.

Yeah, I know—I'm funny, sarcastic, and, let's be honest, kind of an asshole.
But what can I say? I'm **The Devil.**

And this? This is **LA.**
Lost Angels.
Wink, wink. So easy.

93

The cost? A casual $50 billion.

Casualties? Thirty dead.

94

Wherever You Are At

The Year of the Lord

Yep, it's good to just chat sometimes.
Gives you a break from reading, deep thinking, and all that
reflective inner work you humans claim to be so good at. I
know, it's exhausting. Even your God-given gifts have limits.

Also gives me a chance to remind you—ever so subtly—who's
actually running this circus.
I'll try not to read your minds, though I can. I *am* the Prince of
Darkness, after all.
With the title comes a few perks—talents and skills I'm rather
fond of.

Need I remind you? I'm still an angel. Just a... darker one. Dad
prefers the term "fallen," which, let's be honest, is great PR on
His part.

But let's get to the point.
I want to talk, honestly, about why I hate humanity. Yes, a lot
of the chaos I create is just to get back at *Dad*. A little squabble
between parent and child, with global consequences—classic
stuff.

But there are other reasons. Deep ones. Petty ones. Irrational
ones. Deliciously justified ones.

Let's start with your obsession with virtue.

Take Mrs. Wonderful herself—Mary. Yes, *that* Mary.
Mother of the Savior.

You humans worship her in layers—rosaries of every kind. Wood. Plastic. Shells. Draped on mirrors, buried with bodies, hung above cribs. You pray the Mysteries with the persistence of a metronome—the Joyful, Luminous, Sorrowful, and, yes, the Glorious. Over and over again.

But let's skip ahead. The last two Glorious Mysteries? That's where things get... interesting.
The Assumption.
The Coronation.

But we'll pause here. Let's not get me flagged before the real story begins.

Scene change.

She inhales. Slowly. Deeply.
Then exhales. Like something out of a movie.

Four cocktails in—hers discreetly poured into napkins and ice water.
Mr. Needy? Downs six. And a little extra.

A *Xanax*—just a kiss of chaos, slipped into his last drink.

Sara insists they head home. One more round, she purrs.
Another cocktail. Another pill.
LOL.

6 a.m.
The alarm screams. His skull pounds. He's half-dressed, half-conscious, and fully confused.

There's a note. Handwritten. Elegant. Kiss mark at the bottom—green lipstick.

"I hope you enjoyed yourself as much as I did. Till next time. Knock 'em dead."

His workday? Trash fire.
A pot of coffee. A pack of smokes.
The safety inspection? Went *so* well. *So, so well.*

Meanwhile...

Mr. President—Ronald Reagan himself.
You know, the actor who once starred alongside a chimp?

He sets up a commission. Real presidential stuff.

The cause?
Organizational collapse. Decision paralysis.
The usual.

SRBs. O-rings. Cold temperatures. Known issues swept under the rug by NASA and Morton Thiokol.
Ignored. Minimized. Signed off.

The result?

A 32-month delay—nearly **three years** of silence.
Enter: the Office of SRQA (Safety, Reliability, and Quality Assurance).
LMFAO.

Seven of Dad's kids? Gone in a flash—literally.
What was left? Scattered fragments.
Hundreds of careers: incinerated.
Millions of children? Watched live. Scarred for life.

Welcome to adulthood, kids.

Oh, and let's not forget what got you there:
human arrogance.

All thanks to good ol' Dad.

But wait—let me tell you just how *easy* it was...

About the Author

Dr. Sean Patrick Page is a storyteller shaped by the extraordinary. A dedicated medical professional for over 32 years, his life took a dramatic turn after a near-fatal motor vehicle accident—one that left him clinically dead for moments before he was revived.

The aftermath was devastating: months in intensive care, the loss of his career, and the unraveling of his personal life.

Haunted by one question—*Why was I spared?*—Patrick Page turned to a trusted friend, a priest, who gave a chilling yet profound answer: *"Because He's not finished with you yet."*

With time to reflect and a mind sharpened by science and storytelling, Patrick Page began to make sense of a world spiraling into chaos. His academic rigor and personal journey through suffering, faith, and redemption led to *The Devil's Memoir*—a novel where theological insight meets gripping suspense.

Today, Sean writes to challenge perspectives and awaken hearts, inviting readers to see the battle between good and evil not as ancient mythology, but as a present, pulsing reality all around us.